Right Beneath OUR NOSES

And Other Stories

EDITED BY

DAVID ALLAN HAMILTON

DeeBee

For information contact David Allan Hamilton :
davidallanhamilton00@gmail.com
www.deebeebooks.com

Book and Cover design by DeeBee Books
ISBN: 9781896794266

First Edition: March 2019

10 9 8 7 6 5 4 3 2 1

CONTENTS

Kitchen Memories

By Kay Lewis

I GREW UP IN THE 40S AND EARLY 50S IN A GOOD-SIZED CITY in oil rich Alberta. We lived in a pleasant community in a house with a large backyard and enough bedrooms to accommodate most of us. Because of the oil, all our appliances ran on gas – we had a gas refrigerator, gas stove and even a gas furnace. My folks told me that my earliest experience with our gas stove occurred when I sat next to it in my highchair. The family was sitting around the table eating a meal and talking when my mother glanced over at me and noticed I was lying with my head down in my food. At first, she thought I was asleep, but on closer inspection she realized I was unconscious. It appeared that the pilot light had gone out and, as there was no odor to the gas, no one had noticed anything was wrong . . . I guess you could say I was the canary in the mine.

Sunday mornings were my favorite time in the kitchen. That was the day my father took over and cooked us all pancakes. I loved to stand beside him and watch his large hands dropping eggs into the bowl, adding the flour and other ingredients. He had a special way of mixing the batter and he always made it seem like so much fun. We'd then move over to the stove where he had a griddle heating. He made a little pouch filled with salt which he rubbed all over the griddle. Once that was done, he'd drop the batter onto the griddle in absolute perfect circles. We'd stand side by side in comfortable silence watching the bubbles start to form. At exactly the right time he picked up the pancake with a spatula and flip it over. It landed without splatter, no mess and the cooked side would be a wonderful even golden color. At just the right time he'd then pick up the pancake, flip it high in the air and it came down smack in the middle of my warmed-up plate. He was a genius.

Another thing I loved to do with my father was going down the basement with him when he lit the furnace. We had a huge furnace with gas jets in two semi-circles. He turned on the gas, light a long piece of paper which he passed over the jets. The sound of these jets lighting up was so exciting. They made a huge WHUMP! And a beautiful circle of fire grew. I knew that soon the heat would pour out of the hot air registers upstairs and warm the rooms. On cold winter mornings I hung my clothes over a register to warm them up before getting dressed.

We all had many chores to do in our kitchen. My mother and father both worked so, until my grandmother came to live with us, the kids got dinner started and made the lunches. Making lunches was like a factory. 18 slices of bread spread out across the table, margarine swiped across, then mayonnaise, then some kind of meat or egg or something, finally all of them wrapped in wax paper and put in brown bags with each person's name written on them. This was always done at night before going to bed, so all these brown bags would be lined up in the fridge in the morning.

The kitchen wasn't always warm and fuzzy. It was also used for discipline. The door to the outside and the door to the dining room both swung inward and met, forming an enclosure where we hung our coats and scarves on hooks. When my mother had had enough of my doing whatever I was doing to drive her nuts, she'd make me stand behind these doors amongst all the coats. It turned out I had claustrophobia and I stood there and screamed. Of course, my mother thought I was just being difficult. When my sister was bad and sent to stand behind the doors, she just lay down and went to sleep.

I recall my sisters and I standing at the kitchen sink doing the dishes. To make this task seem a little less tiresome, we would sing. Old vaudeville songs mainly. Sometimes my parents would sit at the kitchen table and join in the harmony.

One Christmas my father and us kids decided to buy my mother a new kitchen table. We hid it at a neighbor's house until Christmas Eve. After we finally got mother to bed, we brought in the table and tied a big red ribbon around it with a bow in the middle. I don't know if she appreciated it, but we did.

Our family sat around that chrome table and had some pretty ferocious conversation. Once, when my brother couldn't get anyone to listen to him, he jumped up onto his chair and started yelling that no one wanted to hear what he had to say. The conversations at meal times were no holds barred. We covered politics, religion, ideas, opinions. We were all pretty loud and we loved to talk.

As we got older, my father had to build an extra bedroom, which meant enlarging the kitchen and raising the slanted ceiling, so the bedroom could be built over it. What a mess that was. Trying to work in the kitchen with all the dust and lumber. My grandmother came to live with us, so the house was pretty crowded. But I loved her being there. We came home from school at noon and Grandma cooked lunch. I loved coming through the door and hearing the radio, which was always tuned to the CBC, and grandma would be ironing. The fresh smell of clothes being ironed, and apples baking in the oven was amazing. She knew I loved baked apples with raisins and cinnamon.

Looking back at my life in our kitchen makes me realize how important it was to our family's life and how much I loved it. Except when I was behind those damn doors.

Far And Away

By Jennifer Stolpmann

The cottage filled with smoke and the youngest child coughed and sputtered.

"Da, you're choking us!" Jamie said while cradling the crying baby. "Katie, toss open the door!"

Katie did as she was told, propping the door open with her shoulder against the howling wind. She placed a stone at the base and fetched her bonnet that had flown off and landed too close to the fire.

Archie used his hat to fan the smoke, helping clear the room. The hearth fire had caught too quickly, and the chimney drew too slowly. After a few minutes the smoke dissipated, and the baby calmed. He stood up and reached over to shut the door. The pounding rain had soaked the threadbare carpet at the threshold. He glanced over the fields to Loch Nevis, angry swells cresting white in the storm.

Jamie lay the baby in the basket and gently tucked her in. He moved toward the hearth to peek into the caldron.

"Wha's that, Da? All lumpy and grey." He turned up his nose and went to huddle in the corner with Katie to share the warmth of their bodies. Sadie, their border collie, claimed her spot near Archie's feet and close to the hearth.

"I want Ma's stew." whined Katie, even though in all her six years she had only a few samplings of her mother's stew.

Archie stirred the pot in silence. He had done his best. Out on the croft all day he collected a few turnips and the last of the potatoes on his way back to the cottage. With no meat, he had thrown in some lard and oats to fill their wee bellies. A fresh loaf of bread sat on the table, wrapped in a linen. Christie had stopped by while he was out with the sheep.

"Katie, lay out the table. Jamie, grab some milk for the bairn," Archie's flagging energy making him sound gruffer than he intended.

He scooped out the stew into the bowls and before he could set them down their tiny hands had torn apart the bread and they stuffed bits into their mouths with both hands. He couldn't bring himself to scold them, poor bairns. Hungry and untended as they were.

He picked up wee Maggie and gently tipped the milk into her pursed lips. Her hands reached greedily for the bowl. Archie wiped her mouth and mashed up some stew. He fed her a spoonful at a time saddened by the smacking and slurping of Katie and Jamie across the small table.

"Not so bad, is it? Your mother taught me well." Archie trying, lightheartedly, to give Catherine some involvement in what had become of their family.

When Archie took his first mouthful it was all he could do not to spit it out. *Foul, foul stuff, this is. Goddam woman, where are you this time?*

Every time she returned, he was angrier; less relieved. He didn't want her to come back. Shocked by his own callousness he tried to shake away the shame of the feeling. I must see Father Collins, he thought, confession is long overdue.

A sudden gust of wind blew open the door. She stood in the doorway. The tatters of her shawl and skirts blowing maniacally in the wind. Her matted hair whipped around her bare head as she fell to her knees.

"Mam! Mam!" screamed the children. Sadie ran circles barking. The uproar startled Maggie into another fit of wailing. Not knowing which way to turn, Archie picked up the baby and watched the bairns cling to their mother, all sobbing indistinguishably. The noise rang in his ears. The silent scream that rose in his throat wanted to join the cacophony of pain.

With Maggie settled, he turned to the heaving mass on the floor and gently pried the children away. The smell of filth and urine crept into his nose. He turned his head to reduce the assault.

"Now, bairns. Let's get her up and to the fire, aye." Archie pulled her up by the elbows and led her to the chair. Sadie had given up her spot and was burying her nose in Catherine's filthy hem, whimpering, tail wagging.

"Catherine, Kate. Are you alright?" He had to feign concern. He knew she wasn't alright. And now, he realized, she never has been.

Catherine's head lolled to the side. Archie grabbed her face with both of his hands and looked into her eyes. The dark brown irises swimming in the bright red of her blood shot eyes. He kept gazing, searching, hoping. But they were vacant, staring off over his shoulder. She was away.

* * *

THE NEGLECTED CROFT SUFFERED WHILE ARCHIE TENDED to Catherine and saw to the children. His body rebelled, exhaustion and resentment thrashing together making the simplest chore a feat of endurance. He had to find a tighter rope for his breeches. A worrying cough rattled in his chest. Thankfully, wee Donald down the way had come in to let the sheep out and he and Sadie worked together to bring them back in.

Finally, she was well enough to allow Archie to get back into the field. Her auburn hair neatly arranged in a loose braid, an hours-long task Katie had lovingly thrown herself into. A little pink returned to her cheeks and her eyes saw him, for now. *How long would it last?*

"I'm off now. Won't be far. Send Jamie if ye need me." He firmly grabbed her shoulder, took a final look into her eyes for reassurance, and landed a peck on her cheek.

His shoulders dropped as he sighed. For reassurance, he turned to look back, but she had closed the door. He was out to the field then on to the church. He ventured farther than he should, but his hesitation was overpowered by the need to see Father Collins.

* * *

THE DOOR SQUEAKED AS HE PUSHED IT OPEN. Dust floated in the coloured sunlight streaming in from the remaining stained-glass window. Jesus on the Cross in all his glory. Mary hunched at his feet. Not grand as churches go, but it was a small parish and Father Collins oversaw his flock with a firm kindness met with gratitude, appreciation and generous tithing.

He took his place in the confessional and drew the heavy curtain, releasing more dust into the box.

"Yes, my son." The booming timbre of Father Collins' voice startled Archie. While that voice was inspiring from the pulpit, it was rather unnerving in the confines of a confessional box.

Not one for the niceties, Archie dove right in, quickly, in case he lost his nerve.

"Father, I have wished my wife dead. I have wished that she hadn't returned."

Archie's voice dissolved into a whisper.

"I am so ashamed. I don't love her. I want to divorce her. What shall I do, Father, what shall I do?" Desperation dripped from his plea. Silence greeted him.

A tingle of sweat beaded on Archie's brow.

At last, Father Collins spoke.

"This is a dilemma. There is no easy answer. You well know that I cannot condone divorce, Archie." Compassion softened the priest's voice. "But, you do have a claim, legally, I must admit. You, and the bairns, have been abandoned, and abandoned repeatedly." Another silence.

He continued. "They've seen her in Morar, wondering the path in the hills and her stealing bread. No one takes offence, mind, most feel for her plight."

Archie stared at the dancing dust, speechless, mind whirring. He could, he could. But . . .

"There is a cost, Archie. And not just money, which is significant for a man like you. Think about the village."

Archie picked up on the warning in the priest's message. It was a small village and some things were just not tolerated.

* * *

WITH HEAVY HEART AND HEAVIER LEGS, Archie trudged to the pub. A pint might be what he needed to find some respite.

The pub was quiet. He pulled up a stool close to MacGregor, whose rheumy eyes told Archie he had been there since morning. Stu gave the bar a quick wipe and leaned over.

"What can I get for ye, Arch." He leaned in closer. "It's on the house."

Archie avoided Stu's eyes, his throat clutched as his pride washed away with his breath. Such cruelty in kindness, he thought.

"Ey, there's the Jessie," yelled a voice from the huddle of young men in the corner. "Y'er forgot y'er apron, aye!" The laughter broke out and they all raised their pints. "Taking a break from the washing, are ye!" another voice broke out in a falsetto. "Can't keep the help, eh, Archie!"

Archie's head dropped, the heat of shame rose in his face and consumed his ears. He pushed away from the bar and left the pub, the laughter fading behind him. With his hands pushed deep in his pockets he headed back to the cottage. The shrieks and giggles in the garden greeted him. A semblance of joy softened his heart as he approached. Sadle chasing a stick, the bairns chasing her. The late afternoon sun glistened upon the loch in the distance. A surge of hope fluttered in Archie's heart.

As he entered the gate, the wail pierced his reverie. He stopped. He wanted to turn. To run. Instead, he ran toward the door to see Maggie sat on the floor in a puddle of her own soil. The hearth was as cold as his heart.

"Mam's gone, aye, Da?" asked Jamie coming up behind him, pleading with his mother's brown eyes for a different answer. That it hadn't happened again. Katie sobbed quietly into her small hands.

* * *

THE LAUNDRY HAD BEEN HUNG OUT TO DRY and Christie had delivered another crusty loaf. The sheep were back in and Archie set about with dinner. Mutton stew. The bairns will be pleased.

He took a moment to gaze out at the Loch, inhaling the fresh spring air. He felt lighter.

Wee Donald appeared over the hill, all arms and legs, tearing toward the gate. "Did ya hear, Archie? Did ya hear?" He shouted breathlessly. His skinny arms flailing as he slowed down. Hands on his knees he gasped for breath.

Archie laid a hand on the lad's shoulder. "Take it easy lad," Archie said soothingly. "What's all the noise about?"

"A body." Donald gasped. "A dead body floating in the loch, there is!"

Archie's hands went numb and his arms dropped to his sides. His chest heaved as his breath got away from him.

"Archie, ye ok? Yer face is all funny." Donald looked at him through the dark lock of hair hanging over his eyes.

Blinking and trying to feel his feet, Archie leaned into the stone wall to still the sway taking over his body. "Aye, I'm fine. Just tired, maybe. Now, be off with you now, Donald."

As Donald spun to leave, he bumped square into Jamie, who nearly fell over.

"Da, what's all that?" he asked.

"Nothing that concerns ye," he snapped, causing both children to look at him with surprise.

Recovering he pulled both of them in close and squeezed. They will know soon enough, he thought.

* * *

THEY STORMED THROUGH THE DOOR BRINGING IN RAIN AND MUD. The sleeping children roused by the shouting jumped out of their beds. Jamie ran to grab the baby fearing her basket would be kicked over by the men who had suddenly appeared in the cottage. Katie grabbed a hold of Sadie before she launched herself at the intruders, teeth bared, saliva flying.

"Archibald McLellan, yer under arrest!" Archie's eyes followed the bellow to a small man poised between two brawny strangers. Before he could register, one grabbed his arm and wrenched it behind his back, spinning him the other way. He staggered to keep his balance. Pain shot through his shoulder.

"What? What? Is this? What have I done?" Archie winced as his arm twisted tighter. He heard the clank of handcuffs. The metal cool and sharp against his wrists.

"Da, da!" The children shouted and cried. Katie held tight to Sadie and Jamie had hold of Maggie, oddly quiet in the commotion.

"It's okay. It's okay, now." A soothing purr emerged in the chaos.

Turning his head, Archie saw a familiar figure pushing past the men toward the children. She plied Maggie from Jamie's too tight grasp and gently bounced the baby in her arms. She pulled the children into the far corner and waited.

"Christie!" Archie moaned. "Thank Christ!"

Her blue eyes, glistening with tears, stood tall. Her strength shone in the dimly lit room.

The burly men shoved Archie out of the cottage into the dark night. He turned his head to look back. The crying had stopped. They seemed so small huddled in the corner. As if drawn from Christie herself,

Archie's body tingled with vitality. He felt the blood throbbing in his veins. His heart warmed. All will be well.

11

3 AM

By Seann le

"But Dad, Jack is a murderer!" wailed Alice.

I smiled and looked up from the illustrated book. My kids always amuse me, I love the way they think.

"No, he is not. The giant has all the gold and he won't share. Jack and his mom are poor and hungry," Nate said with a sure nod of his head. The baby fat still there on his cheeks.

Alice threw up her hands in frustration. I imagine a football sailing through the uprights and she, holding her arms just like that, saying, "It's good!" Instead I heard, "It's not the giant's fault that Jack and his mom is poor. And even if it is, it still doesn't make it alright to steal and kill."

She drew out the last word for emphasis.

Nate frowned, pondering this.

Alice sees this and seizes the advantage. She turned towards me waving her brown hair to the side, and said in a confident tone, "We should call the police."

"They won't do anything. Jack and his mother are white, and the giant is not. The cops won't care."

Startled, I stared at them both.

"What are they teaching you in school?" I shook my head. Desperate to change the subject, I closed the book and got up. "Okay, more tomorrow, now brush your teeth."

They both protested. But I'm a seasoned veteran now—a dad with experience.

"You want worms in your teeth? Now go. And I want to smell your breath afterwards, none of this wetting the toothbrushes."

Guilty smiles spread across both of their faces as they hopped off to bed and raced to the bathroom. Everything was a race. I watched them content and grateful.

I tucked them into bed and gave them good night kisses. Then, I made my way to my room and crawled into my bed. God I'm tired, I thought. It had been a long work week. I looked forward to the weekend and sleeping in.

* * *

I WOKE UP LIKE THAT TAVE LO song dazed and disoriented.

"Is it 6am already?" my sleepy brain contemplated.

I forced my eyes open, the room was still dark. I glanced at the clock. It flashed 3:00 am.

"What the . . ." I thought when a jarring noise from my cellphone brought me back to the present. I fumbled for the light switch and managed to turn it on after the second try. I picked up my phone and stared at the screen. Before answering, I stared at the call display.

Brother.

I woke up a notch, more alert now, and thumbed the arrow right and put the phone to my ear.

"Hey Jacob," I said. My voice sounded different, and dry.

"Scott," the voice said urgently.

I woke up another notch.

"Yeah." Then after dragging my voice through a tunnel and stifling a big yawn, "What's up? This better be good." Another yawn.

"Scott. Oh good, you're up. I'm outside."

"Outside?" My brain refused to work at the speed necessary.

"I'm in front of your house." The voice grew desperate.

I glanced at the clock again. It flashed 3:04 am. The red numbers blinked to the rising beats of my heart.

"Alright, I'm coming down."

I checked on the kids and made my way downstairs, stumbling in the dark, leaving a trail of lights on after me. My eyes turned away from the glare. I made it to the front door. I'm fully awake now.

I hope he is alright, I thought to myself as I opened the front door.

He was looking at his grey Acura TL with his back towards me as I opened the door. He spun around at the sound.

I involuntary took a half step back. He looked horrible and smelt worse. His face was pale, his hair in a mess, and his eyes were bloodshot. He was fumigating his mouth with alcohol and weed, but whatever was inside already died.

"What happened?" A sick feeling welled up in my stomach.

He looked at me unsure for a minute, then cocked his head towards his parked Acura.

"I'd better show you," he said, his voice shaky.

He didn't wait for my response but turned to walk to his car.

I grabbed a jacket from the coat tree next to the door and walked out after him. I pulled one sleeve of my jacket on before realizing I didn't have any shoes on.

"Hold up," I said as I turned back for my shoes. Choosing convenience over fashion, I slipped into a pair of old crocs.

He stopped half way down my driveway waiting for me, his hands in his jacket pocket. His body was tight like a drawn bow, ready to loosen anytime.

I took a deep breath as nausea came on and I hurried towards him.

"Remember you told me that you'd rather hear bad news from me first instead of other people?"

I nodded, not remembering, but that did sound like something I would say.

"Okay well, here is the bad news." We stood by his car staring at the trunk.

Part of me wanted to laugh, wondering if all this was a big joke for my benefit. But my lazy brother would never set up something as dramatic as this. Also, I'm not that lucky.

I'm not a pessimist, I told myself as I feared the worst. I'm an optimist with experience.

He took a deep breath and opened the trunk.

A body was inside. A body of a man.

"Oh god."

"Quiet," he hissed.

"Quiet? Are you crazy? This is suburbia! You bring a dead body in a trunk onto my street and park in front of my driveway. And you're telling me to be quiet."

I sounded hysterical

"I know. I know." He almost mouthed the words. He palmed both of his hands face down and frantically gestured me to lower my voice.

"What happened?" I asked leaning in.

"I . . ."

"Never mind, I don't want to know. I don't care."

He stared at me. "I know this is bad. That's why I'm here."

"Why are you here? What do you expect me to do?"

"You are my brother, I expect you to help me."

"Don't you pull that. Don't you dare." I point a finger at him; my eyes glaring.

He made his palm gesture again, and I waved it off but kept my voice down.

"Don't you dare put this on me. This is not like hey bro, I'm short on rent can I borrow a G note."

"I know. I know." He looked around frantically, his eyes wide, his breath short as he scanned my street up and down.

I followed his gaze and did the same. "I live here. These are my neighbours. Do you even realize how this looks?"

I didn't wait for a response. I pointed to the house on my left. "If Cory looks out his bedroom window right now, you know what this will look like. What do you think Cory will do?"

I plowed on, not caring for his battered expression.

"Or better yet, how about my other neighbour," I said pointing at the house at the end of my street. "Chantal walks her dog in the middle of the night because that's what she does; and if she happens to see this?"

My brother just stared at the ground.

"I have kids, Jacob."

He didn't say a word.

My rant was done for the moment as my chest heaved and my breaths came out of me in rushes.

"Shut the trunk. Wait in the car. I'm going to change."

I walked back to the house, not looking at him.

I heard the trunk close, a car door open and shut as I struggled up my driveway like a Sherpa on an Everest ascent. I changed quickly, subconsciously, choosing dark clothing and clothes I won't care if they end up in a garbage bag. I had the sudden urge to kiss my kids as I opened the front door. But no time for that and it's better if they slept.

I closed the front door quietly, suddenly worried about noise. I locked the front door and sped down the driveway eager to get this over with. The passenger side door was locked, my brother gave me an apologetic look as he fumbled with the unlock button at his driver side door. I got in. The car reeked of weed but it was warm.

"Okay what now?" I asked without any preliminaries.

"Ah . . ." he hesitated, eyes wide, "I thought you had a plan."

"My plan? This is your problem, you come up with a plan."

He gave me a pained looked again. I realized I was about to rant again, and it wasn't helpful. I took a deep breath, regretted it. The air in his car stank.

"You didn't come up with anything on your way here. I mean you put him in the trunk. Why did you do that? You must've had a reason." I nudged.

"It happened so quickly . . ." he trailed off. "I guess I panicked. I put him in the trunk, so nobody would see him or me."

"What happened?" I asked, my voice low even though we were in the car now.

"I was in this bar. I went out to the parking lot for a smoke, and there was this chick . . ."

I can see how this is going and I cut in. "Did you do it?" I motion with my head toward the trunk.

He stalled. "Yes and no."

I shut my eyes and balled my hands into fists. "Jacob, this is not one of those times. Did you do it or did you not?" I kept my voice low and even. I'm using every bit of self-control now. "This is just me here. I can't help you if I don't know what's going on."

"I didn't kill him."

My relief was palpable. I let out a long breath that I didn't know I was holding.

"Okay, why is the body in your trunk then?" Seeing his confused look, I waved my right hand as if conducting an orchestra. "Not because you didn't want people to see him. But why do you think they would blame you?"

"I came out of the bar and this dude's body is next to my car. I thought it was a joke at first. You know, haha. But then I thought he passed out. When I tried to wake him, I realized he was dead. That's when I freaked out. I mean, I told you I was out in this bar, this hot redhead and I hit it off. We went outside for a smoke and her psycho ex shows up and starts shouting and spitting at me."

He looked at me expectantly.

I didn't say anything, gesturing for him to continue.

"Well, she jumps in and starts to shout and punch and kick at him. I had to jump in when he tried punching her." He paused and look at me. I remained silent and he continued. "I punched him, and he went down. He crawled away swearing to get even with me and everything."

"Okay, then?"

"Then nothing. We went back into the bar, I tried to laugh it off, but the mood was gone. I just wanted some poontang man . . .you know," he said, his voice pleading.

I nodded to encourage him to finish.

"Well, I didn't want that kind of baggage. I mean that chick was crazy. You should've seen her kicking and punching. So, I left her and went to the car. There the guy was, dead next to my car. I mean the dead guy I just had a fight with in a dark bar's parking lot next to my car. My first thought was go into the bar and get help but I know no one would believe me and with my luck I'll end up in jail. I'm not made for jail Scott. You know I'm not. I don't want to end up being some big guy named Bubba's bitch."

"Did other people see the fight?" I steered him back to the situation.

"Yeah, lots of people. Most were laughing but they all saw us. That's what I mean. I'm fucked. Can you imagine if I went back into the bar or to the cops?"

He looked at me and I looked back at him.

"We need to go to police, Jacob," I said quietly.

"NO! No, we are not. I reek of booze and weed man . . . there's tons of witnesses and some psycho girl . . . I like my ass." His voice rose, a tinge of hysteria setting in.

"You didn't do it. There's a lot of science now. You've seen CSI, they can see that you didn't do it. I mean, if he was shot, you don't have a gun and even if you did, they can confirm it's not yours by the ballistics. Or time of death. Or DNA or other forensics. Everything you're doing now makes you look guilty."

That seem to calm him a bit.

"Jacob, I'll go with you. I won't let them put you in jail," I said, before I thought better of it. I touched his shoulder.

"Remember, you didn't do it. I believe you. I know you wouldn't do something like this. They can't put you in jail for something you didn't do." I paused, catching by breath, letting it all sink in for him. Then I added, "And weed is legal now."

He managed a smirk and nodded after a long beat. "Where is the closest police station?"

I laughed nervously. "There's one near Tenth Line."

As we drive down the silent, deserted streets, time seemed to slow. I heard the thump of the tires over rough pavement.

"If I told you I did it," he broke the silence, "what would've you done?"

I leaned back into the passenger side seat, staring ahead. "I'd chew you out and rant a bit, a long bit, then I'd get you to help me bring the left-over deck stones I have in the backyard and we'd grab one of the old sleeping bags I have in the garage and head to the Ottawa river now."

He turned to stare at me. "For real?"

"Keep your eyes on the road."

"For real?"

I shrugged, still staring ahead. "You are my brother."

Lydia

By Line Labrecque

LYDIA COULD HAVE BEEN DESCRIBED AS A SMART AND A GOOD GIRL. Her loving mother taught her to dance around her distant over-bearing father's outbursts over her mistakes. She never knew what those were before he got mad. Lydia followed her mother's last minute advice to put out the crisis. She could always find a solution to Lydia's misstep.

Lydia also had a grandmother. Seen as an outcast, she often, when no one else could hear, told Lydia to not worry about what her father wanted and to make her own way.

Lydia decided to travel now that she had finished her training. She wanted to know more of the world before she settled in her town. She dreamed of wonderful things for her future and that of the others.

A week before she was ready to leave, the town's dam broke. The waters enveloped the homes, schools and buildings, ripping it all like they were a toy town. Her own home was above the water line and was saved. Slowly the word got out that the accident was caused by a stupid girl who worked at the dam.

Lydia wondered who it was, and if she knew them because she worked part-time at the plant while studying. Her father had gotten her the job. To her surprise, she found out that *she* was being blamed for the troubles. She can't believe what happened. She wasn't even at work the day of the accident. Her father was furious. He yelled at her that he couldn't believe how stupid she could be.

Her mother took her aside and gave her advice on how to take the blame graciously. She was to apologize and admit she made a mistake. Her father will pay for the rebuilding of the town. She can repay him later, somehow. She needed to claim ignorance, incompetence and that she needed his help.

Lydia knew she didn't do this. But she doesn't know who did. And now her city was destroyed, and it must be rebuilt. If she atoned and took the blame, the powers that be, her father, would start the reconstruction, build it all back the way it was. She went to bed with a heavy heart.

During the night, her grandmother stole into her room. She told her that she knew who was responsible and can help Lydia bring the culprit to light. She warned that rebuilding the way it was would not protect them. It would just happen again like it has happened in the past. Lydia was leery of listening to her grandmother. Her father had always called her grandmother crazy, full of nightmares.

Lydia was also afraid that she wouldn't know what to do when she found the culprit. How could she do anything about it? What skills did she have? What right did she have to go against her father's wishes? But she also believed in truth and she knew she didn't do it. She didn't cause the dam to release. She didn't cause the destruction.

So, she decided to follow her and once at her house, her grandmother presented her with a map that supposedly led to the secret lair of the culprit. It was hidden underground. Lydia found the entrance at a cave opening hidden deep in the woods. She imagined dark tunnels with roots sticking out and bugs running over her feet. She took a deep breath and faced the unknown. Her will to get rid of the culprit and clear her name gave her the power to face the fear.

Rebuilding had to be what is more important. While she walked, she began thinking about who, in all the people she knew, would be better able to rebuild and how each person can do what they do best and get it all done. Her thoughts emptied as she entered the opening and she found herself in what looked like a military compound. The cement floor was clean, straight and led to an elevator. Could she call the elevator? Could it be this easy? She pressed on the down button. To her surprise, the door opened. Inside the elevator, she stepped in and the door closed. She heard a hissing sound and the elevator started to go down.

At the bottom, the door opened, and she faced a world she never knew. The roots and bugs she imagined that would be in the cave opening were here, but they were all alight like electricity ran through them. They scurried all over the place, not noticing her, as if answering a silent call from a distant unseen master. Stepping out of the elevator, she heard a faint sound. It was a thumping hum like a very slow heartbeat. It was hypnotizing. She found herself walking forward, steadily as if she knew where to go.

Soon, she saw a figure facing away from her. She couldn't make out who it was. She kept approaching until she was right behind him. A sudden realization struck her and she stepped back out of fright when the figure turned around. Lydia looked up to see her father's wicked smile.

"I see you couldn't keep away. You couldn't do what you were told. Your mother gave you instructions on what to say and what to do. Now, you must pay."

Lydia's mind blurred. She didn't understand anything. Her shock left her thoughts racing everywhere. The world stopped making sense. What was her father doing here? What does he mean? Slowly, Lydia formed the words that her instincts yelled at her. Her father was the culprit. Her father was the person who caused the destruction and her father was asking her to take the blame. Her mind raced, making the connections between how her life had been and what was going on. Her mother always showed her how to respond to the sudden and false accusations from her father and the distant and overbearing presence he had always been. He was always a monster kept at bay with placating responses. If you answered his rages with obedience and humility, then he'd retreat and leave you alone.

Lydia ran back to the elevator. The door opened and as she stepped in, her father said:

"You remember that hissing sound you heard when you entered the elevator? That sound was the a release of a gas that will kill you when it is mixed with the air outside the elevator. You can run away but you will not make it past the next five minutes. I'm sorry that you have to die like this but my plans, my life, my existence are more important than a mere girl. Even if she is my daughter."

Lydia stopped dead. What could she do? Then suddenly she felt a weight in her pocket. Something that wasn't there before. A mask. She realized the mask had appeared to let her escape. She could use it when she got outside. She was about to run away when a bug ran over her foot. She should be afraid, but she noticed the vacant expression on the bug, the blind obedience. And she felt for it. How terrible was a life when spent blindly serving another's purpose.

She couldn't leave yet. She had to find a way to protect the bugs and the people in the town. She had to clear her name. But she couldn't bring herself to kill her father. He must be stopped. But not with his own destruction. His powers had to be rendered obsolete, so that he couldn't dictate, overpower the others. He must become equal to her, a partner in the rebuilding and not the dictator that he was now. He must willingly or unwillingly relinquish his power over people. But how?

Lydia knew her father prided himself on being very smart. Maybe she could outwit him? She offered to play a game, a riddle. If he won she would take the blame, make atonement and go on with things as they were. If she won, he would rebuild the town, take the blame and share the power.

The father agreed, thinking that he couldn't lose. His arrogance was great, and he didn't think a young girl that he trained in obedience could outwit him. Lydia grew suspicious of her father. How will I make him keep his word if I win, she thinks? Then the bug she noticed before came to her. It stopped just behind her and whispered, "Lydia, I felt that compassion for me. I will help you. I'll record the riddle game, I'll show it to everyone on the outside and you can use that to prove that you won. Helping you will help me. I don't like this life. I want to be able to decide what I do myself. I want to go home and help my children." Bolstered by the help, Lydia asked her father, "Shall we begin? I'll give you two chances to answer the riddle I am thinking of. I'll write down the answer before you start."

Lydia asks, "Where does your downfall lay?"

The father thinks on this and he answers. "My downfall would only be possible if another man would come in here and with an army come and kill me. And I know full well that is not possible because no one knows I'm here."

Lydia answers, "No, that is not where your downfall lies."

The father says, "Wait, you are a tricky one. I have another chance." Secretly, he becomes angry. How can this little girl outwit him? *Not possible, I am great. I have been ruling over the land for ever. The destruction I cause is to make everyone adore me when I fix the problems. In that way, I always remain the benevolent master, the one who knows all that is needed.*

Then the father continues, "The answer is nothing. There cannot be a downfall. I have total power over things. I have made life as you and everyone else knows it. You could not imagine another way. I will never fall."

Lydia looked at her paper. She peeked at the bug who had recorded all the conversation and transmitted it to the town hall's screen. Everyone saw it. When he gave her the nod that all was well, Lydia answered her father. "You lose, father. Your downfall lies in your arrogance. You say that no one knows where your lair is and still I found my way here. You say that it would take an army to expose you and yet one of your worker bugs helped me diffuse this game to the outside world. You are exposed, father. Your downfall lays within yourself."

"That is fine, but you cannot survive once you reach the top. That gas will kill you," he spits. Lydia knew there was no guarantee but remembered the mask in her pocket.

"That may be, but your reign is done, and I'll take my chances that someone will help me." With that she took the elevator up to the surface. The bugs followed her out.

Once she got to the surface, she put the mask on and stepped out into the light. Her grandmother waited for her. She had a skin patch with the antidote for the poisonous gas. She applied the patch and took the mask off. Lydia drank in the air and went home to rebuild her town.

Dying Embers

By Ann McKerrow

By Ann McKerrow

Ellen picked up the ringing phone.

"Hello. This is fine. I'm just sitting near the window and looking at the wind whip the leaves off the trees. Yes, I know a place where we could get coffee after our class. It's called the Zebra and it's right around the corner from our building. Ok, see you then." She returned the phone to its cradle and walked over to the fireplace and used a black tong to push a log farther back.

"Who was that?" Mike asked from the rust-colored sofa near the front door.

"Someone I met in class."

Mike threw his car engine repair manual on the oak floor. "Another priest? A guy who thinks you're a nun? I don't get it. First my mother had the priests telling her to have more kids one after another and none of us getting enough attention and second my wife takes courses with priests. I've no use for any of those guys." He watched Ellen walk out of the living room and followed her into the kitchen where she filled the cat's bowl with water. She sat at the small kitchen table and looked out the side window at the neighbor's garden.

Suddenly, a smear of red came into focus. Jeremy the neighbor's son in his red jacket raced across the yard. Other red-cheeked children followed him. Will I ever get to have a child, she thought. Mike was staring at her from his position against the fridge. He kicked the cat's ball into the dining room.

Ellen picked up a pen and started writing out a grocery list. Mike took a beer out of the fridge and snapped it open. "What's that," he asked?

"It's a grocery list."

"Oh, I thought it was a list of what you wanted out of life. Number one, a baby; number two, some guy to support you…"

"Shut up! Just because you're satisfied with your life doesn't mean I'm satisfied with mine."

Black Jack the cat jumped up on Ellen's lap. She stroked his fur and he purred. She remembered the struggle with Mike to even have a cat. Mike had kicked Black Jack off their bed when he was a kitten. Was it an accident as Mike had said or not? She remembered the kitten's broken leg and how it had been a life-saver for the kitten that the small bedroom closet had a window. The vet told her it was vital that Black Jack be in an enclosed space where he couldn't jump up or down or use his broken leg much. She removed all the clothes from the small closet and put the litter box in one corner and his water and food bowls in another. It was Spring, and the open closet window provided sunlight and fresh air.

Ellen put the pen down. "Would you please sit down so we can talk? I want you to know that the guy who just called seems nice and just arrived from Canada. And he's not a priest."

"I don't feel like sitting down. I just want to know what your intentions are."

"Ok, you want to hear my intentions? I feel he is a special person. I feel that he may be interested in having children. And I feel that he would be a good father." She rubbed her forehead. She said more than she wanted, more than she realized. She felt unmoored like she was casting about for a safe port in a wind-whipped lake. All she had was her own rowboat. But was it enough?

"Why did you sign up for a class on the introduction to classical music?" Mike asked her as he kicked out a chair to sit on.

"Because I need more in my life. We've been married 7 years and you have made it abundantly clear that you're not willing to change your mind about having a child and I'm not getting any younger."

"You got that promotion to head office in Baltimore. Isn't that enough for you?"

No, the wheels of the train keep chanting *baby, baby, baby,* she thought. None of the books she read distracted her enough to stop hearing the clicking of the train wheels. *Baby, baby, baby.* Yes, she kept saying to herself, more than anything in the world I want, yes, a baby.

"You remember our agreement?

"Yes Mike, I remember our agreement not to have children, but I was a different person then. We have the house and good jobs and I want to have a child."

"But I don't and never will. You should be happy with your life." He took another beer out of the fridge, put it on the table and left the kitchen. When he returned he tried to find his place in the car repair manual.

Ellen was angry. "Well, I'm not happy with my life, something is missing, and taking all the courses in the world isn't the answer. And going to therapy isn't the answer either. And you're looking for whatever solutions to your car problems infuriates me. Why? Because you're so darn interested in finding solutions to problems with things like cars and lawnmowers and don't care about finding solutions to our problems."

Mike's face reddened. He threw the empty beer can into the sink. Ellen felt some drops of beer on her head. Mike stood up. "I don't have a problem. You have a problem. What if you had a kid with a problem when he was born? What if your baby had no brain or no eyes or no ears or..."

Ellen put her hands over her ears. "Stop shouting at me! I would deal with her or him. As you know, my wanting a child is not something I just thought of this week-end. I've thought long and hard about it, especially on the hour-long train rides to Baltimore and back again every day. But it was you who convinced me to take that promotion to take my mind off having a baby and also by the way, it hasn't worked out at all. I've been taking the trains for almost a year and I've been cooped up in an office for the first time in my life. I liked my life as a health inspector out in the field much better than being stuck in an office doing paperwork like a fly caught on sticky tape."

She continued. "I don't know the future but I'm willing to take a chance on finding what I want rather than crying every time I see someone with a new baby. I'm almost 32 so I don't have a lot of time left on my biological clock to have a child before I'm 35."

"You're stuck with me and you know it. We can go on trips, get another car, a bigger house."

"For what? You're never here. You're always out running or seeing your clients in the evening. I feel I'm at a crossroads in my life."

"You'll never find anybody better than me. Just continue taking your courses and have coffee with all the priests that end up taking the same classes you do. Continue working on your master's degree. What the heck do you think life is really about? It's getting a good job and having a nice house. That's my life, so there!" He walked through the dining room to the living room, opened the closet and grabbed his jacket and slammed out the door. The slamming of the door caused the fireplace damper to close and without the air from the chimney, the fire went out.

Ashes To Ashes

By David Allan Hamilton

"There must be a mistake," Alice whispered.

She stared wide-eyed at the gunmetal urn. "Who would play such a nasty, cold-hearted trick like this? Stealing Bill's ashes? How could this happen?" She scratched her head in the late morning rain, puzzled by the empty canister.

The events of the past week flashed through her mind. Bill failed to get up on time Wednesday morning and Alice, knowing he would be late opening up the Dairy Queen, padded down the hall to their bedroom to rouse him. But the moment she entered the darkness that somewhere between 5:00 am and now, her husband of 32 years had drifted into death.

Alice hauled the chair up and sat beside the bed where Bill's corpse, now covered in a bluish tinge under the bedside table lamp, lay so peacefully. He'd soiled himself, of course. She'd have to do emergency laundry. She smiled quietly in the murky depths of her mind. What would actually seeing her husband die be like? How would she handle the last breath, for example?

But all that mental rehearsing was for naught, because now, he had simply gone. Old Bill wouldn't be waking up any more, and the mix of shock, disbelief, and resignation caused her to look at the body not so much as a philosophical problem to be solved, but as a practical outcome of dying.

Three days later, Bill's ashes sat in this beautiful urn, its mosaic patterns and gentle colours dazzling her. She kept it on her kitchen counter near the coffee machine, an odd place for it, perhaps, but there wasn't any room on top of the piano and she wouldn't keep it in the bedroom that's for sure. So, the kitchen it was.

Then this morning, she gathered it up, drove out to the Dairy Queen where Bill had been the manager for the past twenty years, and prepared to honor his wish that he be scattered in front of the drive thru window. A small group of employees gathered outside in the cool spring air. One of the assistant managers with a missing front tooth, who'd worked with Bill for years, said a few words. Alice could never remember his name. A couple of young counter girls with grease-fed acne cried silently and stared at their shoes. And that's when she opened up the urn and found it empty.

Who had access to the urn over the past couple of days? No one she could think of. The stupid kids were all gone and on the other side of the world now and wouldn't come home just to scatter dad's fart-filled ashes in a parking lot. Waste of money, they'd say. Anyway, they weren't around to pull this prank.

So, who came over to the house? Neighbours with food and sympathy, the reverend, a couple of old employees who'd worked with Bill and just wanted to feel a connection. Perhaps they could have bathed first. Her sister with a long beak stopped in for an afternoon to help clean. Didn't say much, just grunted and pecked around the place. Definitely wasn't her. But of all the visitors and smarmy do-gooders in her home, no one came anywhere close to the urn. It wasn't exactly the kind of objet d'art that one examines in someone else's house.

Alice shrugged her shoulders and turned her face away from the raw wind. She had nothing more to say, and the toothless assistant manager then guided everyone back inside. Burgers needed to be prepped, bananas and cakes to haul out of the fridge.

Later that afternoon, Alice sat by herself in the kitchen with a cup of tea watching people strolling along the sidewalk. Something familiar, some vague memory inched its way into her mind. The ashes were still here. Yes, Alice had taken them out of the urn a day ago and put them . . .

She drained her cup, pushed herself away from the table, feeling the creak of dampness in her knees, and waddled off to the bathroom where she ran the hot water and got undressed.

Then she remembered.

In the counter drawer sat a new cake of soap. Lye soap. The kind she made as a kid at her grandmother's knee from fat and ash. Alice picked up the cake and held it to her nose.

93 Maple Lane

By Erin Forget

It was about quarter to seven at night when I made a left onto Maple Lane, my old stompin' ground. I used to call this place home. The mighty maple trees from my childhood were once permanent fixtures on this street. Now they seemed smaller or reduced to stumps left to decay on the lawns of dated homes.

As I glanced at the houses as I drove by it was apparent that the siding was severely faded. The bright, future-loving luster I remember the neighbourhood having had vanished. And I couldn't help but feel this lament for the past as a pinch in the pit of my stomach. As a kid, the future had all the answers, it was safe. I used to dream of what my life could be. We didn't have much. My father pissed away all our money on booze and was emotionally abusive, but I had my mom and I loved her dearly. I miss her. She loved history and spending time at the library and museum. She would often secretly help local families with their genealogy and sometimes people from overseas would write to her in hopes she could help locate family members that immigrated to the area. On occasion she asked me to help her go through old microfiche at the library to search for names of people, but not to tell Dad. It was our little secret and sometimes she gave me a few bucks to go see a movie if the people she was helping would pay her. As long as she was home in time to prepare a hot meal for dinner, Dad wouldn't get angry. I enjoyed sharing this secret with her, and Dad was probably too drunk to ever figure it out before he died of a heart attack almost a decade ago.

I was on a mission to visit the house I grew up in. Who lived there now? Would they be nice? Did they have a family? Who stared at the ceiling I used to stare at some thirty years ago as I lay awake worrying about what the next day had in store for my mom and me? Did they worry too? I hope they didn't have to worry and I sure the heck hope they were nice, 'cause I'm about three minutes away from knocking on their door and asking them a very odd question.

I felt a sense of loneliness when I recognized the landscapes of yards, houses and contours of the street that were the backdrop to the first eighteen years of my life. It hit me that I wasn't going to walk through the door of my old house and see her smiling face.

I looked to my right and there it was, number 93. The house still had cast iron house numbers spelling out *ninety-three* in cursive, as opposed to the actual numbers every other house displayed above their garage door. The driveway asphalt was cracked in multiple places, the paint half chipped off the wooden garage door, but the umbrella tree my Mom planted still stood tall to greet you as you passed by. It was a modest bungalow, but spacious for a family of three. As I pulled in the driveway I felt a wave of nausea come over me. What if I didn't find what I was looking for?

I parked next to a light blue Toyota Corolla. It wasn't new or old, just a vehicle that faded into the background. I put my car in park, switched the ignition off, climbed out and shut the door gently behind me. I was mindful not to alert anyone that may be inside the house.

Here we go. I needed to know if what my mother showed me from beyond the grave was true. I walked along the keystone brick pathway. Clover and moss peeked through the cracks. Walking past the umbrella tree with a half-baked smile, I could feel Mom's presence. It was comforting. It was mid-June, so the sun was still out. I for sure didn't want to go knocking on a stranger's door in the dark.

I stood on their welcome mat with my figure floating over the doorbell. I pressed it. I didn't hear anything. I waited fifteen seconds in case someone did hear it and was just getting up from the couch or kitchen table. I didn't hear any movement, so I opened the screen door and knocked two solid knocks on the steel door. Nothing. I stood there for about a minute, and assumed no one was home.

As I turned around to walk back to my car, I saw the umbrella tree, and something told me to walk around to the back yard. Fine. My last attempt for the day would be to see if anyone was perhaps enjoying the summer evening on their patio. It felt weird poking around a place I knew so well, but felt foreign at the same time. I followed the interlock around the side of the house and as I gently unlatched the dark green three-foot chain-link gate, I said, "Hello, is anybody home?" Just as I finished the sentence I rounded the corner of the house and a young woman no older than thirty-five sitting on a patio recliner look over at me with a startled look on her face and immediately closed the brightly coloured magazine she was readying.

"Sorry." I said, "I didn't mean to startle you." I made sure not to stand too close, so I kept a fifteen-foot distance. "My name is Jonathan Wrigley. I actually grew up in this house." The worry in her face left and she gave me a slight grin.

"Hi Jonathan, I'm Sarah, nice to meet to meet you." She glanced down at the bassinette beside her to ensure her baby was still asleep. From what I could tell it was a fairly new baby. It didn't look like it could be more than ten pounds. She hastily looked back to me. "Oh, you're JW! You're the one who carved your initials into the bottom left wood panel in my daughter's closest." She proceeded to tell me how they just painted the nursery for their daughter and noticed the carving. "It's still there, now just covered with a coat of white paint."

I couldn't help but smile. "Guilty, that was me. Sorry about that. I was a young boy who didn't value a home's equity. It's nice to meet you too Sarah. Anyway…" I continued, "I don't want to be a bother or take up too much of your time, but I have a small request." Sarah seemed nice, and receptive to what I had to say. "My mother passed away recently from a stroke. It was sudden and unexpected." Sarah responded with sympathy. I added, "She didn't have much and was living in a small apartment. She didn't have a will, and I don't need anything from her, but I am looking for closure. She sacrificed everything for me. She kept me safe. And I never really understood everything she did for me until after she was gone. After the funeral and looking after her estate, I couldn't shake this feeling there was something I could still do for her."

Sarah gave me her undivided attention. It was hard to see but her eyes look watery. She probably had all these new emotions as a new mom and could empathize with my story. I go on. "Last week, my mom came to me in a dream. She was in a house that we lived in for twenty years, this house, and she was in her bedroom, sitting on the bed smiling. I knew she was okay, and I felt better, but then she started to point at the floor. She wouldn't stop pointing at the floor where her nightstand was. And then I woke up."

Sarah looked empathetic and curiously asked, "I'm guessing you're here to visit that old room?"

Yes, yes, I was, but I had no idea if my mother actually left anything in that room. We hadn't lived there in twenty years. The new homeowners could have done renovations, replaced all the flooring. I responded, "Yes, if you wouldn't mind."

She stood up, placed her magazine on the table next to her chair and gently picked up her sleeping little baby. Trying her best not to wake her. He voiced turned to a whisper. "Alright, follow me, but be quiet, I don't want to wake Ella." That's a cute name I thought.

We entered through the patio doors, and the kitchen almost looked exactly as I remember. Just new appliances and a different dining room set. It reminded me of Mom and made me smile. As we quietly stepped through the hall, I ran my hand along the walls. The ceiling felt lower, and it wasn't as spacious as I remember. First, Sarah stopped at my old bedroom, Ella's new room, to lay Ella down in her crib. I peeked in the room, but it looked nothing like my old room. Sarah partially closed the door and then I followed her to the master bedroom. She told me not to mind the mess, but I didn't think it was messy at all, just a few clothes lying on the bed that needed to be put away.

The configuration of the room was a little different and there was a different colour of paint on the walls. I remember the room being a robin's egg blue, and now it was beige. Sarah had a chair where my Mom's nightstand used to be, I asked her if I could move it. She seemed excited to be on this journey with me, and nodded her head. I shifted the chair over, and knelt down on the hardwood floor. It was still in pretty good condition. I softly touched each board to see if there was any wiggle. It was all solid, but as a slid closer to the baseboard I felt a slight movement in the board. Sarah couldn't take her eyes off me as I pressed the piece of flooring until I was able to wedge my finger under it to pry it out. My mouth went dry, sweat beaded down my back. I pulled the piece of wood out and handed it to Sarah. I didn't break focus as I continued to look at this small rectangle gap in the floor. It was dark, I pulled my phone out of my pocket to use the flashlight. It was tight, but I saw an edge of an envelope. "Sarah do you think you can try and reach this thing I see; my hand is too big."

"Of course!" She knelt down opposite me and reached her dainty wrist into the dark space. Using her fingers to explore, she felt something. "Got it!"

Stunned, I watched her pull the discoloured envelope out of the hole. She handed it to me. "I believe this is what you came here to find, Jonathan."

It felt like an eternity as I sat there and read, "For my dearest Jonathan." My mom sent me here to find this envelope. Knees weak, I slowly stood up. My mouth was still dry. I opened the envelope and there was a letter folded neatly inside with smaller pieces of paper around it. As I pulled out the letter I could see the smaller paper had stamps on them. I didn't think much of the stamps, I was focused on the letter. It was delicate and fragile like my mom before she died. I carefully unfolded the paper and read.

My dearest Jonathan,

I truly hope you are the one reading this letter. I need to tell you I'm sorry. I'm sorry for not being stronger and giving you a better life. I was afraid to leave your father. I'm sorry he treated you the way he did. You didn't deserve that. You were just a little boy. I wanted to give you a loving home, and I tried my best. I just wanted you to know you are the best son a mother could ask for and I love you so much.

Love always,

Mom

P.S. These are some stamps I've collected over the years from the different people who wrote to me from Europe asking me to help them locate their family here in Canada. They were different, so I hide them away from your father, so he couldn't sell or destroy them. Perhaps they are worth a little bit of money and you can sell them to treat yourself to something nice.

I lost track of time. Here I was standing in front of a stranger facing my emotions head on. My eyes welled with tears, but they were happy tears. Out of the corner of my eye I could see Sarah on her phone while rifling through the stamps.

"Holy crap!"

My attention was torn away to her. "What?"

"Your mother left you a fortune. This ugly red octagon stamp is worth over nine million dollars!"

My mind tried to process everything that was happening. This couldn't be real. "It said there's only a few remaining in the world, but only one has been found."

I hastily grab the envelope back and look inside, and there it was, a deep red octagon stamp mixed amongst regular stamps by comparison.

"It's called the British Guiana's One-Cent Magenta."

The silence was broken. The front door opened and slammed shut. "Oh crap, that's my husband, you better get out of here. He doesn't like when I have people over without him knowing."

There was frustration in his voice, a tone I wish I wasn't familiar with. We rapidly left the room, and I was met by this tall, mean looking dude in the hallway. I felt if I could explain why I was here I could defuse the situation. But nope, he was pissed, and his anger was directed at Sarah. I couldn't leave her, especially with a newborn in the house.

"Sarah, what the fuck is going on here?"

"Nothing, this is Jonathan, he grew up in this house and his mother left him a letter she hid in the floor boards over twenty years ago. He needed to come find it. Look!" She snatched the letter out of my hands.

His eyes quickly scanned the letter and threw it back at me. "Whatever, you shouldn't have let him in the house without me. Are you stupid?" Sarah looked at me and apologized for her husband's behaviour.

He seemed to calm down, walked to the kitchen and grabbed a beer from the fridge.

Ella started to cry so Sarah quickly scooted to the baby's room. I softly thanked her for her kindness and apologized for causing any trouble. Sarah's mood changed. "It's fine, we're fine. Please, it's best if you go now. I showed myself out the front door and closed it gently behind me.

What had just happened? All I could think about was Sarah and Ella, and wondering if they would be okay. I swiftly walked to my car, opened the door and frantically looked for a pen. I found one and took the envelope in my hand and scratched out *For my dearest Jonathan* and wrote *To Sarah*. I took the letter and stuffed it into my back pocket as I walked back to the house to put the envelope with the stamps into their mailbox. Sarah will find this envelope and she can make a better life for her and Ella. As I turned around and saw my Mom's umbrella tree I smiled and had a feeling everything would be okay.

Determination Of An Athlete

By Deidre Matthews

I KNOW IF SOMEONE HAD TOLD ME TO TRUST MY GUT INSTINCT, I would have laughed. Why? Because usually the root of the problems come from those so called "experts" in their field. They go to school for years to be where they are, so you automatically get the feeling you should trust them.

On March 18th. 2019, it was my 26th birthday. Usually a birthday is a time to celebrate. But frankly that was not today. If anything, it was the complete opposite. I wound up in several waiting rooms of many medical professionals.

The first doctor I saw that day was the lab technician at the Radiology clinic in Delson, Quebec, where I got some emergency specialized X-Rays on my entire spine.

As I was in the waiting room at the radiology clinic, I was remembering a week prior, at the final competition of the season. I had minutes to decide if I wanted to compete or withdraw due to the continuous stabbing sensation in my spine.

I stood beside the ice with my new coach. He gave me a speech of what to remember, while also trying to calm my nerves. While there was not much competition, I still needed the points.

A few minutes before my warmup, I excused myself to the bathroom. In reality, I just wanted to take some codeine.

I turned around gulping the last bit of Gatorade and noticed he stood at the door about to say something. He stopped and switched the subject, "You still haven't had it checked out?"

I shook my head and rushed past him to the ice, barely making it in time for the start of my warmup.

I skated in circles and then I went to see him. I was the first to skate, so we limited the elements.

I was up first. My name was called. He hugged me, and I went to center ice.

I stood in position and fifteen seconds later my program started. It was an easy start and I was flowing through each element. Until about midway through the program when my legs went numb.

I stopped for a few seconds, hoping the adrenaline would kick in. But forcefully continued through the pain and numbness. I had one jump left. I was done. I lost sight at my take-off and it awkwardly felt like I didn't jump. I finished the program and became somewhat angry at my body and the pain I was in . I wanted to be normal. Like I was many, many years ago.

"Ms. M." Suddenly, I was brutally awakened from reliving the competition.

I followed the technician into the examination office.

She had me stand on a wall, with my eyes watering up with a mixture of the pain, the stress and the lights beaming into my retinas.

Every image was taken in an excruciatingly painful position.

After the last one I laid motionless.

The biggest warning sign that something was not right came when the technician helped me off the X-RAY table and handed me a CD. "If your doctor is working, I want you to bring this to him. He needs to see it."

My heart skipped a few beats. I text messaged my doctor and got a response almost instantly telling me it was okay to bring the CD.

I drove to Saint Constant. Which is maybe 8 minutes away from Delson. I stopped in the parking lot and took a few deep breaths. I walked in and there were two people in the waiting room. The doctor was still with a patient, so I sat there holding my phone and the CD.

I guess my body had been noticeably shaking because when he came out he pulled me into his office, ignoring the other patients.

I sat on the examination table lightly kicking my feet back and forth.

He followed me in and shut the door. He made sure I was okay before taking the CD from my hands, "Go home, try and relax. I will look at these images. Come see me tomorrow."

I stood up and he patted my back, "You know we will get through whatever is on these images, right?"

The next morning, before my appointment, I jumped on the ice. I skated in circles doing small elements. My primary coach came up to me and knew something was wrong. I kept playing it off to a point he left me alone.

The moment of truth came. I was at the doctor's office yet again. There were two patients still ahead of me. He came into the waiting room, called both of them into his office and then sat down beside me. "We need to have a serious talk."

He patted my leg and then went to deal with the other patients. I sat there, and my heart was skipping some beats.

While waiting for him to be done with his patients, I did everything in my power to schedule as many doctor's appointments as possible.

After thirty minutes of agonizing hell, he called me into his office. I sat there staring blankly into space. "You need to decide if you want to skate next season. Because the images I have, show otherwise. You have a lot of recovery and therapy ahead of you."

I flashed back to that final competition of the season standing on the podium. I finished in second place.

He was looking at the doctor's report again and said that the damage to my spine was more physical than a birth defect.

I took a deep breath and rolled my eyes. He noticed.

Monday, February 5th, 2018 I was on my way to work. I was on highway 15 going towards the Dix30 in Brossard. I merged into the left lane, when I hit a patch of black ice. I did two or three 360's before realizing I lost full control of my vehicle. I had just enough time to make sure I was far enough from other cars to turn my car so that the passenger side would get hit and not the driver's side. After I hit, I managed to get enough control to pull over. The next thing I remember was being placed on a backboard, with a neck brace, being wheeled into an ambulance. My car was getting towed. Once I got to the hospital, they took the backboard and the neck brace off. The doctors only checked me for a concussion, once that was cleared they sent me home.

He shook his head at the incompetent doctors for not checking more than a concussion especially since it was a total loss.

With everything that was missed my spinal cord shows parts of scoliosis curves. My L5 on my lower spine is glued to my sacrum and my pelvis is no longer in place.

It's been a few days since I was told all this news and my brain has erupted like a volcano. If I am forced to give up this sport I don't know what I would do with my life.

Figure Skating has been a part of my life for 21 years. Competing has been a part of my life for the past 8 years. I was a Provincial champion in Dance and a Vice-champion in Freestyle three years ago. I went from that to having a season and a half of collapses and injuries before I was able to start building back up again in January 2019.

I adore my coaches. One I have worked with for the past five years and pretty much restarted me from scratch when I was diagnosed with Fibromyalgia and Endometriosis. He also saw other diagnoses including Ankylosing Spondylitis and Osteoarthritis. He was by my side for several following injuries. He helped me continue my love for the sport. He helped me beat every obstacle. He is the reason I am where I am today.

There is my other coach who I started with in January but have grown up with in the same club for the last twenty years. He's great and was the greatest addition I made in a long time. Because of him my points started going up for the last half of the season.

I don't know where I will be in a week or two from now. Or even in a month or a year. I don't know what these results mean. Am I frustrated? Yes. Do I want to give up? Yes. Will I give up? No. Am I physically drained? Yes. Am I mentally drained? Yes.

I just know that I need to continue beating all odds. I need to prove to myself that 20 years on the ice was not for nothing. I can't let my coaches down. I can't let everyone who supported me down.

Most importantly.

I can't let myself down.

Right Beneath Our Noses

By Kanwulia Amoye

IT ALL HAPPENED SO FAST. Ali and I were walking home from school. We did not like to get on the bus as we were just outside the school bus radius, but we liked to walk and talk and enjoy our newly found freedom in middle school. Our parents gave their permission so long as Ali and I always walked together, we had just gone past the bend on Rock Haven Lane when we heard a boy scream as he was pulled into the woods. In the split second when Ali screamed, "Run Addison!" I found myself running down the hill in the direction of school. There were not too many houses in the locality, and we only slowed down when we saw a lady holding a green plastic watering can and tending to her very beautiful garden. Mrs. Jade, as we discovered was her name, asked us why we were running so frantically down the road. Words came tumbling out as Ali and I tried to explain what had just occurred.

Mrs. Jade was stunned, and she asked us to come in with her to call the police. She ushered us into her spotless kitchen where she called the police. We could hear her explaining the situation to them, and she came back to us to tell us the police were on their way. She's such a sweet old lady, she gave us some paper napkins to wipe our tears and she tried soothing us as she told us that everything would be okay. The boy would be found as Rock Haven is such a small quiet town with little or no crime. Mum and Ali's parents were on their way. Mrs. Jade had called them for us also.

She told us to go into the living room and make ourselves comfortable since the police and our parents were on their way. She also offered us some cookies and Kool-Aid. We were still visibly shaken but she spoke so nicely to us that we sat down and relaxed. Ali nudged me and pointed towards the portrait of her family and a picture collage of her son's different stages of life which dominated one wall in the living room. It seemed ominous to me. The wall was filled with her son's pictures. Mrs. Jade came in smiling. She said she could see us admiring the hodge-podge of Henry that she had on the wall. She said he drowned in the lake behind her house when he was twelve years old. He was such a good swimmer and she never understood what happened. She took a photography class some years ago and decide to make a collage of Henry's pictures on her wall, so she could see him all the time. I thought it was nice and I told her so.

The police came in to question us. Officer Malone asked us to describe the person who grabbed Tony Brown. Ali said that she had only seen a hand come out through the woods. As for me, everything was a still a blur. Officer Malone left his card and told us to call him if we remembered everything.

Mum and Ali's parents came in at about the same time as the police. Mum kept hugging me and crying at the same time . . . it actually made me feel better. We noticed the patrol cars in front of the Brown's house. Mum slowed down as we drove past, and I could see Mrs. Brown sobbing. Mr. Brown was trying to pacify her, but he looked quite shaken himself.

* * *

MUM DROVE US TO SCHOOL TODAY. She asked me to get on the bus in the afternoon as she did not want to be worried about me. She said, "No parent should go through what the Browns are going through right now. It is so difficult to be in a position where you have to wonder if your child is dead or alive."

Ali got out of her dad's car right behind me. We held hands as we walked into school.

Principal Geoffrey asked us all keep the Brown's family in our thoughts and to pray for Tony's safe return, and then someone began to cry from the junior elementary. I don't know how I was able to pay attention in class that day, but I was so glad after the last period of Geography. Mum's black sedan was parked right beside the school bus, she said she had taken the afternoon off and so Ali and I hopped into the back seat and asked her if there was any news. We all rode in silence although we both turned around to looked back though when we drove past the spot where Tony had been taken only the day before.

Officer Malone waited in the driveway as we drove in. He wanted to know if we remembered seeing a dark green sports utility vehicle parked around the corner on the lane. Mrs. Jade said she had seen one there and he wanted us to corroborate her story. We both shook our heads and Mum told us to go into the house. I overheard Officer Malone tell her the first twenty hours were crucial to the search, since Tony's chances of being found alive decreased as the days went by... I didn't know when I gasped and began to cry. Ali joined me also, and Mum held us both. Officer Malone left.

The search continues for Tony Brown. Our little town of Rock Haven was seriously shaken. Someone came into our safe little community and snatched him in broad daylight. Our safe haven has been disrupted; parents will not let their children out of their sight. It's really not funny being under Mum's watchful eye all the time and now grandma is here to be with me after school while Mum is at work.

Ali and I were sitting in the backyard when we heard the phone ring, so we ran inside. Grandma said it was the police. A man had been caught, his car matched the description given by Mrs. Jade. He had come to carry out some electrical repairs for someone down the road, but he couldn't find the house, or so he claimed, so he had driven around the area several times. None of the residents had called a repair man so he was taken into custody.

Mum came home still looking sad. She shook her head when I excitedly told her that the kidnapper had been caught. She said that he was going to be released as the was no evidence against him. Mrs. Brown had even cried and begged him to give her back her baby, but he said he did not take Tony.

It was the fourth day since the ugly incident occurred. The suspect was released, and Tony had not been found. Geography class was really boring. Almost everyone was dejected so Mrs. Tranny said we could have the class out in the forest as part of forest school. We were all happy to be outside, but we were all still sad.

I got held back for thirty minutes after school hours because I whacked William across the face in forest school for putting a bug in my hair. I do not know why I reacted so badly. I know he didn't mean any harm.

Ali waited outside for me as usual. We had missed the bus, and Ali was worried about walking and wanted to call her dad. I didn't want Mum to know that I got into trouble, so I convinced her that tragedy couldn't happen twice at the same place. The kidnapper had probably gone someplace else. I did not let her know that I was scared though.

It was a nice quiet afternoon. I stared at Mrs. Jades house as we walked past. Her car was not in the driveway, so I figured she was out on errands. Ali walked briskly. I knew she wanted to get past this lonely stretch quickly. It was then I thought I heard some scratching sounds behind.

I grabbed Ali's hand and as we tried to run, we both heard someone call for help. We looked at each other and Ali said, well let's go get help then but I said the person needs help now so let's just take a peek and run off once we see any sign of danger. I could see the hesitation in her face, but I was happy when she nodded and reluctantly came with me. We walked around Mrs., Jade's exquisite garden to the back of her house. The sound was louder now. It seemed to be coming from the basement.

"Are you okay? "I managed to stutter.

"Is that you Addison?"

"Tony! What are you doing in Mrs. Jades basement?" I exclaimed as I ran over to the back door. I tried it and it was locked. Then all three of us froze as we heard Mrs. Jade say, "Nosey children never come to any good," in her sweet little voice.

We had not heard her drive in or sneak up behind us. I tried to duck but she held on to the both of us very fast. There was no getting away from this one. Ali cried as Mrs. Jade took us down to her basement and locked us up with Tony while she muttered some stuff about meddling children as she went up the stairs. I asked Tony how he had been faring and he said Mrs. Jade treated him nicely and she called him Henry. It was then that I remembered the picture collage of her son in the living room, and how there seemed to be a striking resemblance between the two boys. Mrs. Jade came back with ropes and asked Ali to tie me up while she held a gun to her head. Then she tied Ali up by herself.

Ali tried hard to swallow her sobs because our dear sweet Mrs. Jade had threatened to shoot us if we did not stop the ruckus, when I heard the doorbell ring. Mrs. Jade came and stuffed rags in our mouths, I heard her turn the key in the lock and go back upstairs. Then I heard Mum call out my name, her voice couldn't have sounded any sweeter. I did not know whether to cry as I could not call out with the rags in my mouth. Then I heard officer Malone call out and then unlock the door.

Mrs. Jade was put in handcuffs and taken to the patrol car. She says she only wanted to hug her Henry one more time. Mrs. Brown held him tightly and cried, and Mum cried also. She said she was glad she put a tracking device in my watch because she worried about the way I used to wander off.

Neighbors gather around, and everyone was disturbed because

Mrs. Jade was such a sweet neighbor who was always there for everyone.

A B O U T T H E EDITOR

David Allan Hamilton is a writer, teacher, and publisher living in Ottawa, Ontario. He has edited and published numerous collections of stories from writers attending the Ottawa Writing Workshops since 2017, through DeeBee Books.

David has enjoyed a career with the Federal Public Service and has been a contract instructor at Carleton University. He holds a B.Sc. (Honours) degree in Applied Physics from Laurentian University and a M.Sc. in Geophysics from the University of Western Ontario, and has undertaken literary studies at the University of Sheffield. His own stories often combine his love of the physical world and the possibilities of science fiction. His first novel, *The Crying of Ross 128*, was published in 2018. His second book in that trilogy, *Echoes In The Grey*, was published in March 2019.

You may wish to contact or follow David at the following:

Davidallanhamilton00@gmail.com
davidallanhamilton.com
deebeebooks.com
ottawawritingworkshops.com

@DAHamilton
Davidhamilton1261
Facebook.com/ottawawritingworkshops

Acknowledgments

This collection of short stories would not have been possible without the energy and enthusiasm of the Ottawa Workshop writers who contributed their talents to it. These stories emerged from a one-day writing blitz held in Ottawa in March 2019. Participants wrote and revised their stories over the day, which were then collected and compiled into an anthology and published.

Thanks for reading! If you enjoyed this collection, please add a short review on Amazon and GoodReads!

Reviews mean a lot to writers, so I encourage you to support our growing writers' community by taking a few minutes now to rate this collection and write a few words of encouragement about it. And please share your copy of the book with others!

www.ingramcontent.com/pod-product-compliance
Lightning Source LLC
Chambersburg PA
CBHW022122050726
47591CB00002B/898